Friday's Journey

written and illustrated by

KEN RUSH

Orchard Books · New York

Orchard Books, 95 Madison Avenue, New York, NY 10016

Manufactured in the United States of America. Printed by Barton Press, Inc.
Bound by Horowitz/Rae. Book design by Mina Greenstein.
The text of this book is set in 15 point ITC Symbol Medium. The illustrations are oil on museum board
reproduced in full color.   10   9   8   7   6   5   4   3   2   1

Library of Congress Cataloging-in-Publication Data
Rush, Ken. Friday's journey / written and illustrated by Ken Rush.   p.   cm.
Summary: When it is time for seven-year-old Chris to leave his mother and go to his father's house for the
weekend, he rides the New York subway with his father and thinks about the wonderful places in the city they
can visit together.
ISBN 0-531-06821-8   ISBN 0-531-08671-2 (lib. bdg.)
[1. Fathers and sons—Fiction. 2. Subways—Fiction. 3. New York (N.Y.)—Fiction.]   I. Title.   PZ7.R8954Fr
1994   [E]—dc20   93-4871

To CHRISTINE

It's Friday, and when the doorbell rings I call, "Dad's here."

"Did you remember to pack everything?"

"Sure, Mom."

"Do you have clean socks, a change of underwear?"

"Yeah, Mom."

"How about your toothbrush, honey?"

"Dad bought me a new one to keep at his place." I grab my backpack and open the front door. Dad gives me a huge hug, just like he always does. He jingles a bunch of stuff in his pocket.

"I bet I know what you've got, Dad!"

Dad laughs as he holds out a whole handful of stuff: his penknife, a big bunch of keys, some change, and . . . a bright new subway token.

"'Bye, Mom," I call.

"See you Sunday, kiddo."

I used to be afraid of the subway when I was little. I would stand over the grating and hear the strange noises and feel the warm air coming from down below. I thought that monsters lived down there. But now that I'm seven, I'm not afraid anymore.

Now I'm old enough to use my own token.
I stand on the platform without holding my dad's
hand. I listen to the sounds of the tracks.
   Click . . . ping . . . click . . . .
   I see the eyes of the train glow in the distance.
I feel its warm subway breath blow against
my face.
   "TRAIN COMING!" I announce.
   My dad holds me tight as it rumbles
into the station.

"STOP!"
I command,
and it does!

"OPEN!" I tell the doors, and they do!

I march to my usual place right in the front of the car, where I have the best view of the tracks. Dad watches out the front window, too. "He's just like a big kid!" Mom always used to say.

I grab the door handle. It's the train's throttle, and I'm the engineer.

"ALL ABOARD!" I call.

"FULL SPEED AHEAD!" says my dad.

I push my throttle all the way down.

I can take my train anywhere.

"Slow this express down, Mister Engineer. That's our station up ahead!"

"Yes, sir!" I pull the throttle up, and we screech to a stop.

"So, Mister Engineer. What do you want to do this weekend?"

"I want to go to one of those places, Dad."

"Which ones, Chris?"

"You know, the ones where we used to go with Mom."

We stop, and Dad looks up for a minute.

"You know, Dad, like the park where we used to have picnics, or maybe the place with all that armor, or that dock where we used to watch the ferryboat?"

"Well, Chris . . . I don't see why not. We might even pack a picnic and head for the subway. Just the two of us. That sound okay to you, Mister Engineer?"

"Yes, sir!"

"ALL ABOARD!" Dad calls.
"FULL SPEED AHEAD!"
I shout as we take off up the block.